Amana at School

Written by Megan Borgert-Spaniol

Illustrated by Rob Parkinson

GRL Consultant Diane Craig,
Certified Literacy Specialist

Lerner Publications ◆ Minneapolis

Note from a GRL Consultant
This Pull Ahead leveled book has been carefully designed for beginning readers.
A team of guided reading literacy experts has reviewed and leveled the book to
ensure readers pull ahead and experience success.

Lerner Publications
An imprint of Lerner Publishing Group, Inc.
241 First Avenue North
Minneapolis, MN 55401 USA

For reading levels and more information, look up this title at www.lernerbooks.com.

Main body text set in Mikado 24/41
Typeface provided by Hannes von Doehren.

The images in this book are used with the permission of: Rob Parkinson

Library of Congress Cataloging-in-Publication Data

Names: Borgert-Spaniol, Megan, 1989– author. | Parkinson, Rob, (Robert Anthony), 1971-
   illustrator.
Title: Amana at school / written by Megan Borgert-Spaniol ; illustrated by Rob Parkinson.
Description: Minneapolis : Lerner Publications, [2023] | Series: My world (Pull ahead readers.
   Fiction) | Includes index. | Audience: Ages 4–7. | Audience: Grades K–1. | Summary:
   "Amana enjoys making different crafts at school. Illustrations and decodable text will
   engage younger, emergent readers. Pairs with the nonfiction title My School"— Provided
   by publisher.
Identifiers: LCCN 2022008692 (print) | LCCN 2022008693 (ebook) | ISBN 9781728475929 (lib.
   bdg.) | ISBN 9781728478845 (pbk.) | ISBN 9781728483504 (eb pdf)
Subjects: LCSH: Readers (Primary) | LCGFT: Readers (Publications)
Classification: LCC PE1119.2 .B672 2023 (print) | LCC PE1119.2 (ebook) | DDC 428.6/2—dc23/
   eng/20220309

LC record available at https://lccn.loc.gov/2022008692
LC ebook record available at https://lccn.loc.gov/2022008693

Manufactured in the United States of America
2-1009272-50622-3/1/2023

Table of Contents

Amana at School

Amana makes a tree
at school.

Amana makes a house
at school.

Amana makes a bug
at school.

Amana makes a boat at school.

Amana makes a car
at school.

Amana likes to make things at school!

What do you like best about your school?

Did You See It?

boat

bug

house

Index